Chapter 1

Darius

All I remember is gasping and looking up. The person was gone. I tried to move but then I felt a burning sensation in my stomach. I had been shot. This person just shot me in my stomach. What the fuck? How did this happen? I just wanted to get in and see Jayla. That is all I ever wanted to do.

Breathe. I had to remind myself to breathe but it was getting harder. I had to calm down. I just had to, but that wasn't easy either. I put my hand on my stomach and looked at my fingers. They were covered in blood and I could feel more escape. I got to stop the bleeding. I got to stop the bleeding and I got to calm down. If I do this, I'll make it. I've seen it happen on TV all the time. People bounce back from gunshots like this and even worse. Just the other day someone was shot in the leg and they made it. Another person got grazed and they made it too.

D0126448

I heard a door upstairs open and then close. It was probably Jayla. Good. She'll help me. I'm going to make it.

Jayla

Seeing Darius lying in a pool of his own blood stopped me cold. His car window was broken into and there was some glass on the floor.

"Oh my God!" I shouted. "Darius!" I started to panic. My heart started to beat faster and my palms got sweaty. I reached for my cell phone. "Okay, don't worry Darius. I'm calling the police right now."

"I'm not," he groaned. "I'll be fine."

"Good." I called 911 and gave them my address. "Hold on okay. I just called them and they are coming. Just hold on."

I walked over to him and saw that he was having trouble breathing. He was trying real hard but the wound was too big. He kept gasping for air. He looked over at me. I held him in my arms and laid his head across my chest. "Hold on baby. Hold on, please." I was begging him and God.

"I'm fine." He must have read the panic on my face. "Don't hurt," he whispered, but I knew he was lying. The blood was still coming out of him and he still couldn't breathe.

"Just hold on and stay with me okay. I love you." He gasped again. "I love you Darius." I felt the tears burning out of my eyes. They were running down my face. "Just stay with me."

"No pain," he whispered. He then started saying some nonsense. He was blubbering something but I really couldn't hear him.

"No, no. Save your energy baby, don't talk." I suggested rocking him back and forth. I kept looking around. Where the hell was that ambulance?

About two minutes later, I started to hear the sirens. They were coming nearer and they would be here soon.

"They're almost here. You're going to make it." I looked down and he was breathing much slower. He looked a bit relaxed. "Darius?" His eyes rolled over to me slowly. He tried to move his mouth to say something but nothing came out. He tried to do it again, but still nothing. He was breathing even slower now. Every now and then he would stop and then start. I held him tighter and rocked back and forth some more. "Hold on, they are so close. Just hold on and you'll make it baby. I know that it's hard, but they are almost here. Don't let go. Please don't leave me." He then let out one sharp gasp. His eyes rolled from me then to the back of his head. He was quiet.

I felt his body go limp. He wasn't breathing anymore. His hand fell to his side and hit the ground.

"Darius?" I shook his body a little but I got no response. I shook his body again, but still I felt nothing. I tried to open his eyes, but there was nothing there. "Darius!" I screamed. "Darius!" I shouted again, but still nothing. I knew what this meant but I didn't want to believe it. The lights from the ambulance and police cars were finally here, but it was too late. He was gone.

The workers got out of the car and approached me. They saw the pool of blood and backed away for a second.

"Oh my goodness," the woman with glasses said to the worker. "So much blood."

"Let's get to work," her co-worker said. They approached me but I didn't move. One of them held Darius' wrist. He was probably looking for a pulse. He turned to the lady and shook his head.

"Can we..." she started talking to me, but I didn't budge. "We need to work." I still didn't move. What was the point? I knew that he was dead. He was dead before they even got here.

"Ma'am?" One of the officers said to me. "Can you let them get to work?" That's when I snapped. I just turned up and looked at the cop.

"He's dead!" I screamed. "Because you guys came so fucking late, he's dead!" I put his body down and stood up. The second I did that, the workers went over to Darius. Once again one of them checked for a pulse but he shook his head. The other one took out a stethoscope, and she shook her head. I turned back to the cops. "I called you and he was still alive and now he's fucking dead. It's all because of you!" I yelled.

"Calm down," he put his arms up. "Oh my gosh, she's covered in blood," he told the other officer. "Ma'am, I need you to come with me so that I can get a statement. I know that you're in shock, but we need all the help we can get so that we can solve this." His words then started to fade away. I saw his mouth moving, but I couldn't hear anything.

I turned back to Darius and saw the EMT people were trying to save him or maybe bring him back to life. They tried to shock him, but nothing. They wrapped up the wound and tried to shock him again.

"She's right," one of them muttered. "He was dead before we got here. There was nothing that we could do," he told her.

"He's not even that warm," she replied quietly, but I could still hear them. "Let's just shock him one more time," she suggested. He shrugged his shoulders. There was nothing they could do. They just exchanged looks and shook their heads. They knew what I knew. They came too late; he was dead. Darius was dead.

The lights from the EMT lit up and soon turned off. They went and turned off the engines. They made a phone call asking the coroner to come and pick up the body. They left Darius on the ground, but covered his body with a white sheet. Some detectives came out of nowhere and started taking pictures of everything. They kept trying to talk to me but no matter how much I tried to concentrate, I couldn't hear anything. It was like they weren't talking at all. I was now so numb.

Someone took me by the hand and led me to the cop car. They were pointing at my clothes. I looked down and saw all of Darius' blood on me. I was still covered in him. He was dead and gone, yet he was still here in a way. One of them yelled to someone and they brought back an oversized black shirt and a towel. They helped me change out of my shirt and put it in an evidence bag. They dressed me in this big black t-shirt. They wiped the blood off my face.

I never thought my life would turn out like this. As I stood outside on this cold night with a blanket wrapped around me, I watched the two EMTs carrying the occupied black body bag on the stretcher. I couldn't believe what just happened, and I couldn't believe that this was happening to me. One wrong choice became one fatal mistake. All because of one night of fun. One night had drastically changed my life.

The images of meeting Darius just kept flashing in my head. Just he and I dancing; then going to that restaurant to eat my favorite steak, and the times we had sex. I was flooded with nothing but constant memories.

"I love you too," his voice echoed in my head. Then there was the image of him on the ground, bleeding to death. "No pain," he told me. Those were his last words. He told me that he wasn't in pain. That should have been a sign. That meant he was dying and I didn't want to acknowledge it. There was so much more that I could have done, but I didn't. It was too late now.

The detectives went over the scene. They were going over every little detail. They shone the flashlight into his car window where it was broken. They took pictures of it and all around the car. They looked at the pool of blood and took more pictures of that. One of the detectives went to the cops and spoke to the first one that was on the scene. He pointed over at me and they all looked at me. I knew they were talking about me, but I still didn't care. I was still far too numb to even realize what was going on. Darius was dead. He really just died in my arms.

I watched the van that held Darius' body drive away. It was all really over. He was really gone. A tow truck came and hooked itself to Darius' car. It creaked as it was being pulled up, and you could hear the rest of the broken glass fall to the floor. The car rolled over the glass making a crunching sound. Then the tow truck took the car away. The detectives started to remove some of the yellow tape. Everything was happening so fast, I could hardly keep up with it. Time was so weird. Sometimes the minutes felt like seconds and then it would turn around and feel like hours.

The detectives and the officers were huddled up over there talking. They still were looking over at me and then pointing to where Darius' body was. It was clear they were talking about me. I bet they were trying to figure out who was going to talk to me first. Finally, the first cop that talked to me broke away from them. He slowly walked over to me. From the look on his face, you could tell he was trying to see how he would approach me. He leaned over and looked at me. Then he took in a deep breath and let it out.

"Ma'am," he said in a sad and sympathetic tone. He started to open his mouth again, but he sighed.

Finally, "You're going to have to go with the detectives for some questioning. We need to figure out who did this." He took my hand and led me inside a car. "This is the detective's car. He'll be with you in a minute. Then he'll drive you down to the precinct, okay?" I barely nodded to him. "I'm so sorry for your loss." He closed the car door.

I watched him go back to the huddle with his fellow officers. They all looked sorry and sad for me. I know what's going to happen next; they are going to keep trying to find out if I know anything. They're going to ask if I know anyone who could have done this. I already knew who did this though. It doesn't take a rocket scientist to figure it out. I don't have to be Sherlock Holmes to figure out what happened. I mean they already tried to do this before. They tried to kill me and Darius before but we got away. I guess our luck had run out. They probably won't stop until I'm dead.

Maybe after the first time they tried to kill us, I should have went running then. Darius and I should have taken the first attempt on our lives much more seriously. We brushed it off way too easily. Now look, he's dead, and I'm the only one left that knows everything. Shenice has no reason to keep me alive. For all I know, I was suppose to be killed at the same time as Darius and the killer just got reckless. Or maybe I was his target the whole time and he just settled for Darius.

The detectives got in the car. One was a slim black female with a huge afro. She kind of looked like India Arie. She turned to me with a sad face.

"I'm so sorry for your loss," she started. "No one should have to see what you saw." She stopped, waiting for me to talk, but I didn't say a word. I wanted to talk but the words just sat inside of me. When I wanted to move my lips the energy to do it just faded.

"Miss?" The other detective said. He was tall, black, and bald. He had broad shoulders and very bushy eyebrows. "Why isn't she talking?" he whispered to his partner.

"She obviously in shock. Come on, let's take her downtown and hopefully by the time we get there she'll be in a talking mood."

The car's engine started and we were off. I looked out the window the whole time. It was pitch-black outside. It looked exactly how I felt. I just felt dark inside. There was nothing left in me. I could still feel Darius' body go limp in my hands. I saw his eyes roll back and when it got quiet enough, I heard his last gasp for air. He was trying so hard to live but it didn't matter now. He was gone. He's dead and he's never coming back.

What's going to happen now? What will happen next? Are they going to come after me too? They might. Just to shut me up they might come and kill me. And what if they succeed? What will happen to my little brother Keon and my little sister? Who will take care of them? No, I have to make it. I don't have a choice.

My life was supposed to be so different. I thought I was going to end up with Darius and we would be a happy family. He would divorce his wife and everything would go from there. He would start helping out with Keon. Keon would have that positive male influence that he needed. With Darius' help, I might have even got Keon into college. Then one day, we would have had children of our own. I wanted to be his wife and give him children, but that dream is gone too.

What do you do when the life that you had all planned out is taken away from you? And it's not like it was taken away because Darius and I broke up; he was murdered. There's no coming back from this. Although I changed out of the clothes, I could still smell Darius' blood. Even though he was gone, it was like he was still here.

"No pain." His words were playing over my head. "No pain." I cried as the car went on. Hopefully where Darius ended up, he really was in no pain. My heart ached at that fact. I guess I was still in pain.

The car pulled up in front of the precinct. I looked up at the medium size building. The cold night air hit my face and dried what little tears I had left. I had to be strong. I had my little brother and sister to think about. I couldn't forget about them. As much as it hurts to lose Darius, I can't lose myself in the process.

"Are you ready?" the female detective asked. I nodded my head and followed her lead into the building. I knew exactly what to do.

Chapter 2

Shenice

"It's done." His gruff voice ended the call. I was shocked at what he just said.

"What?" I recognized the voice as Trey, the hit man, but it couldn't be. I thought the last thing I told him to do was to let it go. He looked at me and agreed, so he couldn't have done what I thought he did. I tried to call back but I saw that he called me from a blocked number. I went through my contacts list and tried to call the number that I had for him, but I was told that the number was now disconnected. I guess he did it. I guess he got rid of Darius.

Is Darius really dead? I went to his name on my contacts list and dialed it. It kept ringing and then it went to voicemail.

"Hey honey, I was just wondering where you are and how you are doing. I miss you and I love you. When you can, bring home some milk." I ended the call. I thought that leaving a loving message would make me look innocent just in case Darius was really dead. The police would see that I had tried to get in contact with him.

I can't believe Trey really did it. He might have gotten to Darius. Maybe he just shot him and Darius is in the hospital. But now that I think about it, there is no way that Darius isn't dead. Trey is effective and thorough. The whole reason I hired him was because he didn't make mistakes and he was really good at what he did. If he told me that it was done, I knew what he meant. Darius was dead.

To think it was just some time ago when I got the money together to do this. I knew that once I got the ball rolling, there was no stopping it. That's probably why he would ask me if I wanted to do it or not. I know what I wanted to do. As soon as I decided on a goal, I just did it. That's how I was in real estate, that's how I was in my relationships, and that's how I was when I hired the hit man. Once it was decided, there was no turning back. Darius is gone and that is that.

But what is going to happen to me? What should I do? Where should I go? In a blur and out of nowhere, I started packing up. I don't know where I was going or even what I was doing, but I had to do something. Darius is dead. I thought I would feel joy, but I didn't. I felt somewhat empty now and worse, I was scared. What was going to happen now? Would everything go according to my plan or was it all going to shit?

I looked on my bedroom nightstand and saw a picture of me and Darius with our daughter. We were smiling and happy. She was just born and everything seemed perfect. Everything seemed right. There was no way in the world you could tell Shenice back then of what her future might hold. If someone would have told me back then about all that would happen now, I wouldn't believe them. I probably would have cursed them out and kept pushing on. I loved Darius with everything in me and I was going to fight for him in the end. But after all these years of me fighting alone, the love for me changed. It went down to like and then hate.

How many times have I turned a blind eye to all that he's done wrong? How many times did I have to pretend that I didn't notice that he was coming home late smelling of perfume? How many times did I stand by and do nothing while he disrespected our vows over and over again? Look at what he's turned me into. I was never the type of woman to even go through her spouse's phone, and he had me chasing him down like a dog. He had me becoming a fucking detective. He turned me into something I never thought I could be. And now he's gone.

"Shenice!" Jamar called from downstairs. His voice at first shocked me but then I remembered I just gave him a copy of the key. I was tired of him calling and texting just to get in here. This was very much his home too and now it will be his home. It was nice to see that he was putting that copy of his key to use. Now that Darius is gone, he can actually move in. It might be weird for the baby at first, but she's always loved Jamar. She calls him Uncle Jammy. In fact they have always had a close relationship. So maybe it won't be so hard.

"I'm up here." I called out. I was going into my closet looking for things I could pack up. I tried to decide between my sundresses or skirts. That's when I saw it; the last dress that Darius bought for me. He thought on the last trip he could sweep me off my feet and I'd forgive anything. I can't get really get mad at that. He only did it because that's what worked in the past. Earlier in the years if I was mad at him, he would just buy me things. But now that wasn't enough. I was through with the cheating and all the lies. Darius wasn't going to stop. He was never going to stop. No matter how many times he would tell me that he changed and that he was becoming a better man, I knew that he was lying. He had said it too many times and I was done waiting like a fool. I couldn't convince myself anymore of a tomorrow that was never coming.

Jamar came upstairs smiling. His smile put me at ease. All that racing tension and nerves were just washed away. I was so in love with him and seeing him reminded me that I made the right decision. Looking at him now, I felt no regrets at all.

"Hey babe." He kissed me on the forehead. He looked down and saw me packing. "Are you leaving?" I looked around and saw what a mess I had made. In my panic, I turned this once neat room, into a zoo. They were clothes everywhere. I didn't even realize that it had gotten that bad. I was such in a daze.

"Shenice, what is going on?" He picked up some of the clothes and started to fold them. He tried to clean up most of the mess that I made. I sat down on the edge of the bed. I didn't know how I was going to tell him, but I knew that I had to.

"It's done." I used the same words that the hit man did.

"What's done?" He wasn't catching on.

"It's done Jamar." I gave him a look. "It is done." His eyes started to open slowly. "Yes, it's done. He's gone."

The room was quiet. All you could hear was the water gurgling from the toilet. Jamar had his eyes closed and he was rubbing his temples.

"Really?" he asked. His face changed. You could see that the news was really affecting him.

"Yes." I informed him. I walked over to him. "It's over and it's all done. Now we can start our life."

"Our life?" He looked at me like I was saying something new.

"Yes Jamar, our life. You know what I'm talking about. We've talked about it a million times, you, me, and the baby," I huffed. "We can have this whole new life together, boo. Today is a new day. We don't have to sneak around, and we don't have to feel guilty anymore. It's all over and now we can start."

"Is it even worth it anymore?"

When he said this I cut my eyes at him and he sighed heavily. How could he even speak those words? I've done so much, no, in some ways we both put in work for this new life of ours. Now he's acting like he wants to back out? He's acting like he wants no part of this. Just what is going on? He wasn't like this just a few short days ago.

"Do *you* think it's worth it, Jamar?" I asked him with my arms crossed. "I'll be completely honest, okay? I don't want this to start an argument, I just want to get something off of my chest."

"Go ahead."

"You've been nagging me about us being together and I'm tired of it. Don't you see the lengths that I've gone to for us to be together? I did this for us." I poked him in the chest. "You were always asking me for when it was going to happen, well now it has. Here is the day that it happened. I did it and now we can live." He looked at me and shook his head.

"You didn't need to go as far as you did Shenice. You knew that you didn't have to, but what did you do? You hired a hit man and now Darius is dead," as he said the words I could see in his eyes that he was a little sad.

He and Darius had been friends for a long time. They always joked that they were brothers. Now the person who he thought was a brother was gone. I didn't stop to think of how this would affect him, but I know he'll be fine. It won't take a day or a minute; it'll take some time. But there will a be a day when he will thank me for what I've done. Once we are together and happy, he'll get it.

He pinched the bridge of his nose and closed his eyes. He took a deep breath and then opened his eyes slowly.

"Anyone else would have left you by now," he said slowly. "But I believe in us." Those words made me happier. "You of all people know that Darius was a good friend of mine, but I'd be lying if I said that things weren't different for us. He was not my best friend anymore for the past few months; he was nothing but a business partner. He became someone I ran ideas by and that's it."

"Yes." I went back to packing.

"No, stop. We are not leaving."

Now I looked at him like he was crazy. Of course we had to leave. We needed to pack up everything and go.

"We can't stay here. Why would we stay here? We need to get out of here Jamar. We need to go as far away as we can," I suggested.

"Where would we even go?"

"Anywhere but here."

"But why would we go?" he shot back. "You don't think that it would be suspicious if we left right after your husband's murder?" he pointed out. "If we both go, then the police won't stop until they find us. We have to stay."

"I didn't think of that," I admitted. It was nice to see that he was thinking of scenarios that I wasn't.

"Listen, I have to stay here and play my role."

"What role?"

"I was his business partner. I just can't leave here and let the business fall apart. I have to stay here and take over."

Jamar was right. If he left and the business fell apart, not only would it be suspicious, but also a lot of things would be ruined. A lot of that business has ties to me too, but now that Darius is gone, I think it would be best to leave everything to Jamar. He was really good at it. I could help him with the sales part of real estate and he can do what he does best, the marketing.

I've seen how Jamar has helped Darius make the business what it is. Because of his great marketing skills, the real estate company has seen a lot of celebrity clients. These top-notch clients brought in a lot of money. I know that if the company was in Jamar's hands, everything will be fine.

"Okay," I nodded. "You're right."

"I have to stay here and play my role so no one thinks I was involved, and I will run the business," he repeated this sentence once more. He didn't even hear a word that I said. He didn't even acknowledge what I just said.

"Are you okay?" I asked him as he repeated the last sentence one more time.

"I'm fine," he said, but I wasn't so sure.

He started rambling to himself now. I'm sure he was in shock about all that was going on, but it was still a bit worrying to see him like this. He was repeating things to himself. It was like he was trying to make sure he got it all right.

"Play my role and run the business," he kept saying over and over again. "Just play my role and run the business."

I started to unpack and watch him. He was still going on and on, but this time he sat down on the edge of the bed. When I was finally finished, I put the suitcase away. I was about to say something to Jamar, but I decided to leave him be. It was clear that he needed some space right now, but I was still worried about him.

"Run the business," he was repeating. He had his eyes closed and was rocking back and forth a little bit.

I simply walked to the window and looked out. The sun wasn't even up, but like I told Jamar, it was a new day. But now seeing him acting like this, I don't know...it's a little weird.

"What have I gotten myself into?" I whispered making sure that Jamar couldn't hear me at all.

Chapter 3

Trey

"The police are asking for your help. Last night there was a murder in the parking lot of a condo complex. Thirty-five-year-old real estate mogul Darius Black was killed while getting out of his car. Police have no suspects and there were no witnesses," the news anchorwoman said. I sat back and watched the news carefully. This was a story I was especially interested in.

"All I heard was gunshots. At first I thought it was my TV and I didn't pay it any mind, but when I realized it was close, I just froze. I've never had anything like this happen before," Some fat black woman was crying. It wasn't like I was shooting at her. I never let my gun go off if I'm not precise. After that one mistake where I missed, I wasn't going to do that twice. She was going to be fine.

"That's crazy that this happened here. This is a pretty safe neighborhood. I let my kids out all the time so that they can go to the library down the street. Right now I'm not so sure if I should do that anymore." I rolled my eyes at the white father talking about his kids. His neighborhood was still safe; I just had business to handle.

"Darius Black leaves behind a young daughter and a loving wife. We will have more details as they come in. Next, is there lead in your drinking water? Here's how...." Her voice faded away. I started laughing when she said that Darius left behind a loving wife. A loving wife? Really? If only they knew how much she really loved him. She loved him so much that she hired me to kill him. And it wasn't like she wasn't sure, she was so determined to do it. Even though she told me to back off, she said herself that she was going to do it. I couldn't let that happen. She would have only been sloppy. Then what would have happened? She would have gotten caught and turned around and blamed me. No, once I started this job, I was going to finish it, and that was all.

Flashback:

I had been following Darius for a while now. After my mistake and that little nonsense meeting with Shenice, I knew that I had to finish it. He was really sticking home with his wife and going to work. That wasn't good for me because I really wanted no witnesses and I didn't want Shenice to get in the way. I knew that I had to get him alone and get it done. But for the longest, he kept going home. I kept waiting for him to go back to his side chick's place or maybe just go somewhere random, but he never did. He just went to work and went home.

This is why I don't like taking on kills that my boss didn't give to me. My boss is very clean in what he does, just like me, but he goes above and beyond. When he would ask me to kill someone, he would know all the possible locations where I could do it. There was no guessing or strategizing on my part. Maybe that's why we worked so well together. We were so alike. We like to get the job done and we love to make money. As good as my reputation was, my boss' reputation was untouchable. That's why nobody fucked with him. If someone even whispered something bad about him, he'd send me out to take care of it. But Shenice found me, and I was impressed.

Not a lot of people knew me by my face. Everyone knew my name and has heard stories about me, but no one has ever really found me. The fact that Shenice went out of her way to find me was a good look. When I saw her do that, I knew she meant business. I respected that about her. She paid me for a job and I was going to do it.

Finally one day, Darius started driving somewhere other than work or home. When I saw which streets he was taking, I knew exactly where he was going; he was going to see the mistress. I took a shortcut that I knew so I could beat him there. I was running all types of red lights, but I didn't care. I was taking back roads where no one would see me. I parked across the street from her place and just waited. I put on my black gloves and a mask. I touched my hip to make sure that my gun was still there. Yup, everything was going according to plan.

When I saw his car pull into the parking lot it was go time. I got out of my car quietly and started walking towards him. He was on the phone and he didn't see me at first. When he recognized me, I just rushed towards him. His eyes opened wide and before he could say a word, I took out the gun, and pulled the trigger letting out some shots. He fell to the ground and just closed his eyes. I took my gun and smashed open his car window. I pulled out his tray and took the little bit of change he had there. Then I opened the glove compartment and took out whatever was in there. I looked at what I done, I left the car a mess so that they would think it was a robbery gone wrong.

I was about to leave when I heard him gasp. I looked down and saw that he was still alive. I brought my gun up and was about to shoot him in the head, but I decided against that. With the hole that I left in his stomach, there was no way he was going to stay alive. Even if the ambulance came in ten minutes, he was gone. The blood was gushing out of him. I had to get out of here. I stayed here for too long. I ran across the street. I opened my car door, threw the things I got from his car inside, and then started the engine. I looked across the street and saw that he was still out there alone. I drove off through back roads again and left him there to die.

Five minutes after I was far enough away from the neighborhood, I sent my driver a text message with my location. About twenty minutes later, he pulled up.

"Send this to the junkyard." I took the things that I got from Darius' car. I put it all in the glove compartment. His little chump change, I took it and threw it in the field behind me.

"Make sure that they crush this tonight." I reached into my pocket and pulled out an envelope.

"They shouldn't give you any problems as long as you give them this money. You stay there and you watch them crush this car." I looked at the crappy car that I was having destroyed. "Someone should put this car out of its misery." I joked and he chuckled.

"I got it," he reached for the envelope and gave it to him.

"This is for you," I handed him a stack of cash. "You've been really on your game."

"Just doing what I'm suppose to do."

"Yeah, but I appreciate it."

My driver was dependable but my boss always told me to make sure that he was happy. A happy worker that was making money, you almost always had his loyalty. Not that I would ever get caught, but if the police ever got close to me, I know he would continue to have my back.

"Thanks," he took the money and put it in his pocket. "You gonna take the car? Or are you going to call an Uber?"

"No, I'm taking the car. You can call the Uber from the junkyard. That makes much more sense. Of course you would be calling a ride from a junkyard." I thought out loud.

"Got it." He was about to get in the car and leave, but then I stopped him.

"Wait," I called out. He turned off the car engine. I took off my gloves and opened the passenger car door. I put the gloves in the glove compartment. "You got my change of clothes?"

"Back seat," he told me and I went to the car to change. He even had a paper bag waiting with my new clothes. I saw a fresh pair of sneakers there too in my size. I quickly changed and put all the old clothes and boots into the paper bag. I went back and handed it to him.

"Make sure you scatter this in the car too. That way it will all get crushed. Just don't touch any of it."

"Got it."

"You can leave."

He started the engine and drove off. I got into the all blacked out car, and drove home. I rolled down the window to let some fresh air in. I went to the news radio station. I listened for five minutes, but there was nothing on it about the shooting. That's when I knew that he either hasn't been found yet, or the news didn't get to the story yet. Whatever the case was, it only meant good things for me. I was so thorough there was nothing tracing the incident back to me. Now all I have to do is sit back and wait for them to close the case or send it to cold case.

Present:

Watching the news finally break, I saw that they still had no leads. They will never have any leads. The car was crushed down to the cube and with it, was any evidence. I had my driver go three states away and throw the gun in the closest river, lake, or ocean he could find. He took the picture of the bridge that he threw it over. That was gone too. I had nothing to worry about. I just watched the news so I could hear them say that they were going to close the case. As soon as I hear that, I'll know that the job is completely done. Until that day happens, I'm just going to lay low for a while.

I got up and got back to my original business. I had some pick ups to do and some drops to make. Just because I was laying low doesn't mean that I wasn't going to continue to make money. Making money never stopped, no matter the occasion. But since I was laying low, I had to be smart about it. I texted my driver and told him to come upstairs. Within five minutes, there was a knock at my door.

"What's up?" he asked as I opened my door. He's been working for me for years now, but he's never been in my place. I kept that part of my life to myself. I didn't want anybody to see where I lay my head at night. This was all for me and me only, but right now I didn't have a choice. Right now I had to break my own rules because I needed someone I trust to do some things for me.

"Come in," I told him and started to walk away. "Close and lock the door."

He did as he was told and followed me. He stood and looked at me.

"You can have a seat right there on the couch," I told him while I made my way to the fridge. "Can I get you something to drink? I got some beer, soda, juice, water, whatever you need," I offered going through my fridge. "I got Henny if you want some."

"Nah, I'm good. If anything, just give me a beer."

"Cool." I reached in and grabbed a bottle. I handed it to him and he opened it. He sipped it slowly and nodded his head.

"Thanks."

"I know I never asked you up here but right now I gotta lay low. I did a great job ending that dude, but I want to make sure I got all my shit covered. I don't think that his wife will say anything about me, but you never know. You can't trust females. One minute they pissed off at you, and the next they cryin' over you. I know she hired me, but now that he's gone...I'll have to see how she acts."

"I get it."

"And this is where I need you."

I sat down on the opposite side of the room. I leaned back. I knew that I could trust him, but I didn't like handing over any parts of my business to someone else. Of course my driver has shown me that he can be loyal and think when the pressure is on him, but I liked having my hands on everything. I liked knowing for sure that the work was getting done, but I can't do that right now. I have to stay here and be a boss either through phone calls or text messages. I didn't like that. I was hands on, but I really didn't have a choice.

"I've always told you that I can trust you and now I'm going to need that more than ever."

"Okay."

"I need you to do my drops and pick ups. I need you to be my eyes out there on the street."

"Whatever you need," He told me and I felt more at ease.

"Good, because business is still moving and going. Don't think that there is ever such a thing as a day off."

"Okay."

"Now that I'm here, I need you to be me out there. I need you to handle situations like you're me. If you ever get stuck on anything or if a nigga wanna try you, you handle it like I would. You can text me or call me first to make sure that it's the right decision, but then you handle it. You got that?"

"I got it."

"Good. Alright, let me put you up on game."

That's when I broke down everything to him. He already knew a lot because he's been driving me for all this time, but there was still some to teach him. I taught him how to keep the boys on the corner happy and loyal and how to handle customers who tried to play him.

"Make sure you count out all the money right in front of them. Don't let these niggas tell you that they got the money, you have to make sure it's there."

"Yeah, okay."

"And when you get the chance, watch them. Make sure that they are doing their work. Just every once in awhile pull up in another whip and see what they doing. I don't want niggas that ain't working while I'm paying them. I don't want niggas that's going to be flashy and make shit suspect. If you see that, you handle them. If they try to talk back, you handle them. I don't care if that means you gotta slap the shit out of them or beat them down in the street, don't ever let these dope boys think you soft."

He nodded his head again. I was giving him a lot of information and I didn't have the time to make sure that he got it 100% right. Some of this he was going to have to learn himself. He had to put the work in and see what it was like. As much instruction that I gave him, I knew he would do it his own way, and that's cool. As long as the work got done correctly, I couldn't care less.

"I got it. I got to make sure everything runs like you would do it."

"Exactly," I smirked. "You do got it. Alright, go over to the strip and get the money. You know how much everyone is suppose to give you?" I asked and he nodded his head.

"Good, count it all up. If they doing the work right, bless them with some of the money in this. Just break them off a few bills, nothing crazy. When it comes to the customers, just take the money and keep it moving. Don't be nice, don't smile, none of that shit. Those motherfuckers are the ones that will try to rip you off. If they do that, slap the shit of out of them. Make sure you get the money from all the customers somewhere quiet and shit. Don't be all out in the open."

"Got it."

I thought about it some more. I was about to tell him to start getting product, but I kept quiet. I wanted to see how he was going to do with all that I gave him. If he did well, then maybe in a week or two, he could move product too. Or maybe by that time, this whole shit storm will die down and I'll be back to running things.

"I'll call you in ten minutes to see how everything is going," I stood up. He took another gulp of the beer. I reached out my hand for the bottle. Once he gave it to me, I pat his back, and sent him on his way. Everything had to go good, or it won't be good for him at all. I respect his loyalty and his drive, but that meant nothing if he couldn't do what I told him to do.

Later that night, the driver texted me that he was done. I told him to come up and we'll count the money. I got out the money machine. If everything was right, he should have twenty stacks. It was a lot of money, but I had been putting off these drops and pickups for a while because I was taking care of the whole Darius shit. It had put me off on my other work, but that's not an excuse. I fucked up. When I didn't kill him that night, I fucked up. That's all on me.

The knock at my door let me know that my driver was here. I opened the door and saw him with a black duffle bag. I told him to follow me and he brought the bag to the table. There he saw that I had the money counting machine waiting. We went through the duffle bag and I put the cash on the money machine. I sat down and started counting.

"How did everything go? Anybody give you any problems?" I asked while I took the money out of the paper bags that some people put it in.

"Not really. I had one customer try to short change me, but I threw that nigga on the floor and kicked him."

"Let me guess, the nigga that work by the sushi restaurant?"

"Yup." He shook his head.

"That motherfucker has always been a problem for me." I grit my teeth. I hated when customers tried to disrespect me.

"You want me to put some bullets in him?" he smirked. "That motherfucker got an attitude problem."

"Nah, I'll handle him. He's about to make a big order because he's going to NYC. He has this going away party and he wants everyone there to be feeling nice. I'll take care of him. I'm going to beat the shit out of him." I thought about it. "Nah, I'll pop up in NYC. I need to show him that he can be touched anywhere."

"That might be what it is. He might think that because he's leaving Atlanta, that he can be as reckless as he wants."

"He about to learn real quick that he can't," I laughed. "My reach is long. I'm going to pop up in NYC, and teach him a lesson." I thought about it.

The more I said it, the more I knew I had to do it. "He's been doing this shit for too long."

I went back to counting the money. So far, all the numbers were looking right. I knew that I made the right decision by letting my driver take over for a little while. He was being more and more useful to me everyday. When I finished counting the money, I saw that I was over by one stack.

"Oh, one of the customers said that she wanted to make an order for some pills. She told me that she told you that already," the driver explained before I could even ask. I tried to think and that's when I remembered.

"You talking about the white lady who drives that BMW?" I asked.

"Yeah. She said you can bring the pills tomorrow. She knows that you're good for it."

"If only all of the fiends were like her," I said out loud. "She's always on time with her money and she never give me any shit," I nodded my head. That's when it hit me. He could have easily pocketed the money and I'd never know about it. He was proving just how loyal he was. "I'm going to take care of that tomorrow. I think I can leave to go do that."

I put all the money back in the duffle bag. I reached in the pocket and handed him ten stacks of cash.

"What's this for? You need me to drop this off somewhere?"

"Nah, this is for you."

"You always breaking me off with bread."

"That's because you always puttin' in the work. I never have to check up on you," I told him. "I know you got a young kid. So put this in a college fund, but have your girl do it. Just put little by little and after taxes, put a whole bunch in there."

"Thanks."

"Nah, you earned it. Keep doing what you doing, and I'm going to make sure you never starve. You can go, I got this."

The driver left and I went into the back and put the money away. I had to give it to my boss later that week. Even though I was laying low, I would never miss an appointment with him.

Chapter 4

Jayla

"Okay, one more time. I know that this is a lot, but we have to make sure that we have all the information so we can get whoever did this," the male detective said.

"I understand," I whispered.

"So Darius told you that he was coming over?"

"Yes."

"Did he say what he was coming over for?" the male detective continued.

"He just wanted to see me," I answered him.

"Did he seem upset?'

I paused. I remembered that Darius was upset and I knew exactly why, but I couldn't say it here. If I did, I'd be dead too. Who knows what Shenice would do to me?

"Jayla, is everything okay?" the female detective jumped in.

"May I please have a drink of water?" I pretended to have a dry throat. I made my voice sound raspy and hoarse. As she handed me the cup of water, I quickly took a sip. "Thank you." I sighed. "No, Darius didn't sound upset. He sounded normal like everything was fine." I lied.

"Did he tell you if he had any problems?"

"He didn't have any. He just wanted to see me."

"Did he tell you if he had any enemies?" the male detective kept asking questions.

Did Darius have any enemies? I thought of Shenice. His supposed loving wife. She was his number one enemy and from all that Darius told me, she's been his enemy for a while now. I wanted to say her name, but there wasn't a guarantee that she would be locked up. What if she hid her tracks well? What if she never got charged? Then all that would happen is that she would get out and I would have to watch my back. Or even worse. What if she told Jamar to make sure that I was dead? Then I would have to watch out for him.

"No, Darius didn't have any enemies," I lied once again. "Darius really got along with everyone. He was a friendly guy. I don't know who could have done this to him." I started getting teary eyed again, "I can't believe he's dead." I broke down and started sobbing. The female detective sat down next to me and hugged me. Although I didn't know her, I just cried in her arms.

I was numb earlier and I didn't really cry. I just sat there in shock, but now it was real. Now it was true. Darius was dead and Shenice was the one behind it. Not only Shenice, but Jamar too. Darius always talked about how Jamar was his brother, but look at him now. Now, he's dead because of his so-called brother and his wife. It was too much.

"I think she should go home after this," the female detective told the other.

"Yes, we've asked all the questions we needed to ask. Thank you so much for your cooperation."

"Of course," I sniffled. "I want you to get who did this," I lied again. I did want them to get Shenice and Jamar, but I didn't know if they could make the charges stick.

"We're going to come back here with your statement typed up and all you have to do is sign it, okay?" The male detective got up.

"Okay," I replied. The female detective handed me some tissue. "Thank you."

"Is there anything else I can get you while you wait?" she asked while she had the door open.

"No, I just want to go home."

"Okay. We'll get that statement right away. Once you sign it, I'll give you a ride home."

After I signed my statement, the female detective drove me home. I was quiet the whole ride over but it wasn't long before I drifted off into sleep.

"Jayla," Darius' voice felt warm and loving. I turned around and saw him by our favorite restaurant. "You coming?" he smiled. "Because I know how much your ass love these steaks." He laughed and I joined along.

"Of course." I held my hand out and he grabbed it. He squeezed it and we sat down at our table. The steaks were placed in front of us.

"I know you're happy."

"Of course," I smiled wide and dug in. The steak was just as delicious as always. I playfully rubbed my stomach. "Yum, yum," I joked.

"I'm going to learn how to make this damn steak just for you."

"Why thank you."

Everything was so perfect. Darius looked great, the restaurant was empty so it was quiet, and the steak was delicious.

"How are your brother and sister?"

"Well my sis is enrolled for college this fall. She's taking a summer job though," I said sadly.

"Why do you say that like it's a bad thing?"

"Because that means that she's going to stay there. I want her here with me."

"But you have to let her be independent. You have to let her be her own person. You have done so much for her. Look at what you did with the money you had."

"Yeah, that's right."

He smiled and went back to dinner. That's when it hit me. I never told Darius about the money that I had saved up for my brother and sister. I loved him, but I always kept that information to myself.

"How did you know that?" I asked.

"Know what?"

"About the money."

"What money?"

"You just talked about the money I saved for them. I never told you about the money."

Right then the restaurant started to fade. We were somehow on my couch back in the condo. I looked around. I was home, but I still wanted to know how he knew about the money.

"How did you know that?"

"I love you," he told me with his eyes beaming. "I love you so much that I feel no pain when I'm around you."

"No pain?" I repeated.

"No pain."

Those two words brought me back to reality. I was dreaming. I looked at Darius before me and I knew I was dreaming. The more I realized this, the more he started to change. He went from sitting on his couch to lying on the ground outside. The blood gushed around him and there was that pool again. The huge pool of blood was beneath him.

"No pain," he told me in the same voice he had before. He reached out for me. "Hold me."

"No." I backed away. I tried to move but my feet didn't budge.

"Hold me," he gasped.

"No."

His hand grabbed my ankle and pulled me down. The blood got all over me. He was now in my lap.

"Don't worry," he whispered. "It'll all be over soon."

"NO!" I screamed.

"Jayla..." the female detective's voice rang clear. Someone was shaking me awake. "Jayla! Get up. You're having a nightmare," she told me. I slowly started waking up and I looked around. I was in front of my condo complex. I was home. I turned and saw that she was looking at me. "Are you okay?"

"Am I okay? I don't think I'll ever be okay, but I'm the best I can be for right now," I found myself telling her.

"Do you need any help getting upstairs?"

"No, thank you."

I got out of the car before she could suggest anything else. I just wanted to climb into my bed and sleep. I took out my key and put it into the lock. The condo was quiet and empty. Before I started the questioning process with detectives, I called my cousin and told him to keep Keon over for the night. I didn't want him anywhere around this. I don't think I want him here for a while either. I don't feel safe here, so I really don't want him here. The thought of him being here made me worry even more.

Chapter 5

Shenice

I drove the car to the address that was given to me. My mom sat on the passenger's side and my five-year-old daughter sat in the backseat. She was kicking her legs laughing along to the Disney song that I put on the radio. She was so happy in this moment. I wanted to freeze her just like this. I wanted to remember her happy and unaware of what has happened.

"Did they tell you what they called you down here for?" my mother asked me in a low voice. She didn't want her granddaughter to hear.

"No, the police just called and said to come here." I left out the details saying it was about an identification. I needed my mom to be in the dark. The less she knew, the better.

"That's all?" she pressed on for more information that I wasn't going to tell her.

"That's it Mama," I sighed. "I hope that everything is okay though."

"Why do you say that?"

"I haven't heard from Darius at all."

She gave me a concerned look and I tried my best to look the same. I pretended to be worried.

"I hope that this is not about him, but I can't help to think that it might be."

"Don't think like that," she told me in a hushed tone. "And especially don't say stuff like that in front of your daughter."

"But Mama, what if-"

"Hush up!" she whispered. "You have to have faith. Everything is going to be fine and if it isn't..."

"I can't even think what will happen if it isn't," I said in a sad tone. "What will I do without him? What about my daughter?"

Just then we pulled up to the building. On the front was a sign identifying the morgue.

"Is this the address?" my mom's eyes opened wide and looked scared.

"Yeah. I didn't know that it lead to this," I started to tear up. I mustered all the strength I had to cry.

"What's wrong Mommy?" my daughter asked in the back.

"Nothing baby, Mommy is just thinking about something," I told her looking in the rearview mirror. "Hey, how would you like to hang out with Grandma while Mommy does something really, really boring?" I tried to sound playful. I didn't want her to catch on.

"You want to play on Grandma's phone?" my Mom suggested, trying to sound cheerful.

"But all your games are boring," the five-year-old diva complained.

"Okay, but I just downloaded a new Elmo game," my mom winked at her.

"Elmo!!!" She kicked and laughed. "Okay Grandma, we play."

"Just wait in the building and I'll get to you."

I got out of the car, leaving the keys inside. I knew my Mom would get out of the car and watch my daughter while I did this. I already knew what this was about. He didn't want to say it over the phone but I knew what they wanted. When they called they said, "Just come to this address and a detective will speak with you." When I asked for more details, they just got more secretive and evasive.

"Mrs. Black," the female detective's voice made me jump. I didn't even realize that she was behind me the whole time.

"Oh my goodness," I panted.

"I'm sorry, I didn't mean to scare you."

"Well you can understand if someone is scared coming to a place like this," I looked around. "What am I doing here?" as if I didn't already know.

"Will you please follow me?" she asked. I nodded and followed her lead.

She opened a side door to the building and led me down a pristine white hall. It was clean and felt like a hospital, but it had a distinct smell. That must have been the smell of all the chemicals to keep the bodies from falling apart. There were some huge windows but they were all covered by blinds. You couldn't see into them. One of the rooms had a door open and I saw the rows and rows of what looked like office desks. I knew those things didn't hold any files, they held dead bodies.

"Mrs. Black, I don't know what they told you..."

"They told me nothing," I pretended to sound scared. "What's going on? What's happening?"

"Mrs. Black unfortunately we found a 35-year-old man that was shot to death."

"Okay..." I was pretending to be in denial. "What does that have to do with me?"

"We believe it to be your husband."

That's when I screamed like my life depended on it. I fell against the detective and she caught me.

"No," I was acting like I was a mess. "No!" I yelled. "You're wrong. He's not dead. He's fine. He's probably at his office or working with a client, but he is not dead," I sobbed. "You're wrong."

"That's why you're here Mrs. Black. You have to tell us if we're correct."

She then brought me to a room where there was a white sheet over something. That's when I was really scared. I didn't want to see Darius' body up close, but I knew I had to.

"Don't..." I stopped all of a sudden. "Just give me a minute," I rubbed my temples and took a deep breath. "Okay." I walked over slowly. She nodded at somebody and they pulled the sheet off his face. He looked like he was resting, but he was so pale. His eyes looked sunken in and his lips were black. It was real. Darius was dead as a doornail.

"Oh my God," I whispered. I pretended to reach out for him, but the detective stopped me like I knew she would.

"Is this your husband ma'am?"

"Yes he is," I teared up some more. The tears rolled down my cheek so much that she gave me a tissue. I stood there for a minute or two crying as much as I could force out of me. "Can you take me out of here please?" I asked. They covered the body and wheeled it away. The detective took me out of the room.

The hallway seemed smaller now. Trey delivered on his word. I turned and looked at the room. I saw them put his body away. They pushed it and then labeled the outside.

"Mrs. Black, I know that this is a lot to process but if you don't mind, I need to ask you a few questions."

"Yes please," I whispered.

"Do you know if your husband had any enemies?"

"No, he didn't," I said confidently. "He is a great man. I mean...he was," I gasped and shook my head. "I can't believe he's gone."

"I know this is hard but just a couple more questions."

"Okay."

"Did he tell you if he had any problems with anybody? Maybe an old friend? A client that didn't like the way he handled his business?"

"No, nothing like that."

"Okay." She sighed and then opened her mouth to say something, but she hesitated.

"What is it?"

"This is going to be difficult for you to hear."

"Nothing can be more difficult than finding out that your husband of ten plus years is gone," I replied in a matter of fact way.

"Are you aware that your husband was having an affair?"

That's when I pretended to be mad.

"What are you doing?" I snapped.

"What do you mean?" She was lost.

"My husband is dead and you are going to accuse him of being unfaithful. He was a great man and we loved each other. We never had any secrets against each other. How dare you say that my husband was cheating!" I acted like I was defending his character but deep down inside, it actually hurt to do so.

"It was just a question, Mrs. Black."

"No, it was more of an accusation. Are you trying to tarnish the good man's name?"

"No, Mrs. Black. I apologize if you feel that way but I have to ask you that."

"Why?"

"Because I don't want you to be surprised if this goes to court. We found your husband's body outside the home of his mistress."

I rolled my eyes. I didn't mean to but to find out that Darius was killed outside that whore's house was really the icing on the cake. The little piece of regret that I felt, went away. There was a part of me that actually felt sorry for him, but that was gone. Even in his dying fucking hour, he was still going to be the unfaithful piece of shit that he was. Of course he was found outside that slut's home, where else would he be? God forbid he died on his way home to his family or even on his way to buy something for his daughter. What an asshole.

"What?" I acted as if I was shocked.

"So you didn't know about a mistress."

"No," I was becoming more shocked. "Do you know how long it's been going on?"

"I don't really, but I would have to guess it's been going on for quite some time."

"Oh my goodness," I shook my head. "I can't believe it," I sniffled. "Thank you for telling me."

"It's okay." She rubbed my back briefly to comfort me. "Is there anything you can tell us?"

"No, it seems you guys knew something about my husband that I didn't." I looked at her, "but I would think you'd look into the mistress. She obviously knows something, I mean she was the last person he was with."

"Okay Mrs. Black."

"That's all I can think of."

"Okay. Thank you for you time Mrs. Black; I'll bring you to the exit."

Outside the building I saw my daughter jumping around and skipping. The beads in her hair clicked-clacked as she went on. She laughed and giggled while she was chasing some birds. My mother saw me and gave me a half smile. I shook my head at her to let her know it wasn't good news. She gasped and covered her mouth.

"Mommy!" My daughter came racing to me. I bent over and picked her up. "Are we done?" she sounded so bored and exhausted.

"Yes we are," I gave her a small smile. "Mommy is done with that boring work."

"Good. I want to go home. I'm tired."

"Okay, how about we go to the restaurant and then go home?" I suggested. Her little nose scrunched up.

"Umm...." She held her chin like she was thinking hard. "I guess that's all right."

"Let Mommy strap you in the car."

My mother jumped in.

I got my daughter in the car and strapped her in the car seat. I closed the door and then reached for mine. I opened it and before I could get inside my Mom stopped me.

"Was it what you thought?" she asked in a low voice. I nodded my head. "What happened?"

"He was killed outside his lover's home," I decided to let her in on the details. It's better she hears it from me than from the news.

"What? He was cheating?"

"Yup. The detective wanted me to know so that I wouldn't find out anywhere else." My mom shook her head in disbelief. "It was so hard to see him like that," I whispered.

"He looked so frail and weak," I pretended to be sad. "What am I going to tell my daughter about her father?"

"I don't know," she told me truthfully. " I heard that they have children's books on this. I guess one day we'll have to sit down and tell her he's one of the angels now." She walked over to her side of the car and got in.   Before I got in, I chuckled and whispered, "He was no damn angel." I rolled my eyes.

Chapter 6

Jayla

After barely getting enough sleep at my home, I decided I couldn't be there anymore. It was so hard. When I called Charmaine and asked her if I could stay over, she invited me in with open arms. I cried on her shoulder all night and into the next day and all she did was listen to me.

"Tonight at 10 police still have no suspects for the murder of real estate businessman Darius Black." A news report had just started. Charmaine walked into the room and went to change the channel but I stopped her. I wanted to hear this. "Atlanta police are still asking for the public's help," the anchorman said. Then they showed the front of my condo that was still taped off.

"Darius Black was shot and killed right in front of the building you see here. Police say that he was visiting a friend when he was more than likely approached by a robber. Police believe the two might have exchanged words before it all went wrong," the anchorman finished.

Then it cut to a small press conference. There were cops and the detectives on stage in front of a podium and microphone.

"We believe that this was a robbery gone horribly wrong," one of them said. "The victim's car was broken into and some things were stolen. We think that both the victim and the perpetrator fought and the victim was killed. We still have no leads on the suspect so if anybody out there has information, please don't hesitate to call the police. We are now offering a $5,000 reward for any information that leads to an arrest," the detective added.

"Darius leaves behind a wife and child," the anchorman finished.

The news went on to cover more things. I shook my head in disbelief. It was on the news again. The last time I heard it was on the car radio on the ride over here. They didn't say any names but when they went on with the story, I knew who they were talking about. I turned it off and just drove straight to Charmaine's house. I had to escape it all, but it was even on the TV. There was no escaping this.

"It's so crazy," Charmaine finally spoke sitting next to me. "I can't believe it."

"If you are in shock imagine being in my shoes."

"I can't even," she shook her head. "Darius is...." she didn't say the words. I guess she thought that if she said it, I would break down and become a puddle. I already did a mini cry on that detective's shoulder. After that, I went back to being numb.

"You can say that he's dead. Whether you say it or not, it doesn't change the fact."

"I know that," she whispered. "But it's still fucked up."

Hearing my best friend say those words released something in me. That's when the real flood came pouring out of me. I started to truly mourn. Everything I have been holding back was released in a big way. I felt the weight slowly lifting off of my shoulders, but there was still so much of it left. Darius, the love of my life, was really dead and gone. He was gone and he died in my arms.

"I'm so sorry," Charmaine apologized. "I didn't mean to..."

"No, this is good." I said in between cries. "I haven't really cried."

"I noticed that," she rubbed my back. "You can't keep this all in Jayla."

"But what am I supposed to do? Am I supposed to cry all day and night."

"You cry as much as you need to girl," she held my shoulders. "This is not something you can get over in a few days. You were in love with this man and now..." She slowed down her words. "Now he is gone. And that is sad, and it's fucked up, but you are allowed to mourn."

"But I have to be strong." I cried some more. "I have others to think about. I have others to take care of."

"How do you expect to take care of others if you're not taking care of yourself?"

Charmaine's logic always shined through. She had a point and I knew it. I had to take care of myself. I couldn't just close myself to this. I couldn't just walk around on eggshells about my own feelings.

"I am just afraid that... "

"Afraid of what?"

"That I can never go back home. Not only did it happen there, but there are too many memories."

The day after I spent the last night at home, I just looked around and was surrounded by my memories of Darius. I remembered getting ready for dates, meeting him at the door, or him coming into my bedroom so we could have sex. He was a big part of that condo and I couldn't be there anymore.

"Can I stay here for a little while longer?" I asked sniffling.

"You can stay here as long as you want," she smiled. "Consider this your new home."

After weeks of staying at Charmaine's apartment, I started to feel a bit better. I, of course, missed Darius, but there was nothing I could do about it. He was gone. And mourning him wasn't going to bring him back. I had to find some way to move on with my life. If not for me, for my little brother and sister. I had to be strong for them. They needed me to be there for them.

Work helped a lot with me trying to find a new normal. Even the most boring task helped me in some way. Work was the same old routine, and I needed that right now. I just buried myself in my work and did well. My supervisor Nikki noticed but she never approached me. I guess rumor got around about what happened to me because except for Kim and Charmaine, people avoided me. I had to expect that though, after seeing my place on the news, it was only a matter of time before people put it together.

"Okay Mr. Stewart, I'm going to come back and give you some new linens." I told my 91-year-old elderly patient.

"Take your time dearie, I'm not going anywhere. These legs haven't worked since the 70s," h e joked, and I laughed along.

"Well, it would be rude to leave you without telling you what I'm doing."

"I'm your patient, not your Daddy."

Small laughs like that, helped the day get better. It gave me a little break from all the madness that was in my head. I patted him on the back and made my way out of his room. I brought back his linen and then got his lunch ready. After I served him his lunch, I went to the break room to have mine. I heard laughter but when I stepped in the room, it got really quiet.

"Hey," Kim had been using the same sympathetic tone that I had grown used to. "How are you doing?"

"I'm doing fine. About the same as yesterday," I told her.

"Hey, I'm just checking on you. You know, what you went through..."

"You don't have to remind me," I cut her off. "Thank you for your concern, but I'm trying to get back to my old self, or at least the best version of myself for now."

"Okay."

So they let me in on some gossip. Kim bumped into a reality star while on line at the supermarket.

"He is so fine and I am sorry to say that I acted a fool," she shook her head.

"Off of a guy that use to be on Vh1?" Charmaine laughed. "He wasn't even in the main storyline, he was just the friend."

"Well it doesn't matter," Kim brushed off her comments. "Look at the picture we took together."

She showed us the selfie of them smiling. Well the guy was smiling but Kim was cheesing like a kid at Disney World.

"Girl why are you smiling like a crackhead at Crack fest?" Charmaine snapped and I busted out laughing. It felt good to laugh.

"No, I'm not," she looked at the selfie. "Okay, so maybe I was smiling a bit too much."

"Maybe?" Charamine replied. "Girl you was smiling with him like he was LL Cool J or the Rock. Damn, I'll even accept that if it was Kevin Hart because I know you have a thing for funny chocolate men, but this guy isn't even a celebrity. He look like the dude that cut people's hair."

By this time, I was laughing a bit more. Charmaine was going in and Kim kept trying to defend herself. Leave it to my girls to lift my spirits up, even if it was only for a little while.

We were nearing the end of the workday when I saw Nikki go into the office. She was talking to the human relations director. I knocked on the door and saw both of them looked up.

"Good afternoon Jayla," Nikki greeted me. "How can I help you?"

"Actually, I need to talk to you both," I informed them. They exchanged looks and then turned their attention back to me.

"What is it?" the Human Relations director, Joy, asked me.

"I've been thinking about this for a while, but I got to leave here. I can't work here anymore."

"You want to quit the job?" Joy looked confused. I guess she hadn't heard.

"No, I'd like to transfer out of Atlanta."

The only sounds you heard were the computers.

"You want to transfer out?" Joy asked. "Why would you want to do that?"

"I..." I opened my mouth but Nikki shook her head and cut me off.

"You don't have to say it." That's when I knew she for sure knew what was going on with me. "We'll look into that right now."

"But I'd like to know the reason why so that I can put it in her file," Joy turned to her.

"I'll tell you later," she said under her breath. "Let's look to see where there is another opening."

Joy and Nikki went through the database of the company. Luckily for me I was a CNA at a company that had many other facilities nationwide. So it wasn't like I had to start over someplace new, I could pick up my position and just go anywhere.

"Do you have any preferences?" Joy asked not looking up from the computer screen.

"I don't care where I go, I just can't stay here." I told them. They exchanged looks again and then went back to the computer.

"The only thing we can find is all the way in Houston," Joy let me know. "Is that going to be a problem?"

"No, not at all." It was the first time I had really smiled all day. "Thank you so much."

"We'll put the paperwork in and give you a definite date on when you can move," Joy went on.

"We're going to miss you here," Nikki said as I made my way out the door.

I went back to Charmaine's and got right on my laptop. I started looking for places in Houston. It needed to either be a three-bedroom house or a three-bedroom condo. It had to have enough space for me and my siblings. I went through a lot of listings to make sure I found the perfect place. Whenever I thought I had found the right place, I would use Google maps to get a feel for the neighborhood. If I liked what I saw, I just went ahead and favorited it. As soon as I got my definite date on when I was relocating, I would call the real estate agents that were on the listings.

I had to let Keon in on the plan. Ever since the murder, he's been crashing at our cousin's spot. I know he's worried about me, but at least I knew he was somewhere safe.

"Keon, I'm glad you picked up. Let me guess, you guys are over there playing video games." I rolled my eyes.

"Just a little bit." I could feel him smiling from here. "How about you though? Are you okay?"

"I'm fine Keon," I sighed. "I'm going to get into my car and come over to see you."

"I'll be waiting."

I got to my cousin's place in no time. When he opened the door, I saw that the video games were everywhere. These two were always into video games and stuff. They probably haven't gotten much sleep. The whole place was nothing but games and junk food. I smiled looking at it though.

It was nice to know that Keon was in a place where he felt safe and could have fun.

"Hey," my cousin gave me a hug. "Are you okay?"

"I'm fine. Thank you for asking. Where is my knucklehead brother though?"

"He's getting his ass whupped in some Street Fighter," he laughed.

"Nah, you're cheating. You keep using Ryu, why don't you use someone else?" Keon shot out.

"Because Ryu is the best. Why would I use someone else?" My cousin shook his head. Before I could say anything, he left to go to the other room. He knew it was time to leave us alone.

"So, how are you really doing?" Keon asked me.

"I said I was fine."

"This is me you're talking to. I'm not one of your friends; I'm your brother. I've been living with you for a while now and I know how much you loved that nigga," he sucked his teeth. I shot him a look and he apologized. "Sorry, but you was really in love with him so I don't expect you to be fine."

"I'm as good as I can be," I admitted. "To be honest with you there was a reason that I came here to see you. Yeah I'm checking up on you, but there's something else that I want to tell you."

That's when I let him in on my plan to move out to Houston. I told him how I already put in the request to be transferred. I went on to let him know how I didn't feel safe, especially with Shenice and Jamar still out there.

"Wow, Houston," he sighed. "This is coming out of nowhere but it makes sense. You got to go where you feel safe." He crossed his arms. "And if you don't feel safe here, there's no point in you staying."

"Exactly."

"Besides with all this drama, it's best to get out of here. Like you said, Jamar and Shenice, who knows what else they got up their sleeves? They probably suspect that you know it's them, but I don't think you should stay here long enough to find out."

"That's the point. I don't want to keep having to look over my shoulder. I don't like being paranoid," I confessed. "I just want things to be normal, but I know I can't have that here."

"You can't."

Hearing Keon confirm my fears actually made me feel better. They let me know that I was making the right decision. I had to get out of here. It was the right thing to do.

"I think the first thing to do is to find places out there," he started.

"I already got a jump on that." I let him know about the listings.

"Good and the other thing you need to know is I'm coming with you." Keon revealed.

"Really?"

"Of course, you're my sister," he smiled. "Wherever you go, I go."

I hugged him tightly and then felt relieved. I was so happy that he was going with me. He was right. I had to get out to Houston right away.

"There's one thing we have to do. We have to go back to the condo."

"Why?" I started to panic, but he just hugged me again.

"We got to get started right away. Let's go back and start packing."

I thought about what he said and nodded my head. He was right. There's no better time to get started than right now.

"Thank you," I told Keon. "Let's go back."

Chapter 7

Shenice

Sitting in my chair dressed in all black, and pretending to be sad about Darius was exhausting. Everyone kept coming over to me and consoling me, and I had to act like I cared. I wasn't sad for Darius at all. He got what was coming to him. He was a cheating and lying dog for years and he was finally put down like a dog. I may look like a wreck on the outside, but in my heart, I wasn't really sad at all. I was just so happy and satisfied that I got away with it.

I'm so glad that I hired Trey. When I went looking around for someone to take care of Darius, I knew I had to find the right person. I didn't want some amateur that was desperate for money and wouldn't do the job right. I wanted a professional. So when I heard whispers of a guy that could go in and out, without a trace, he sounded like the perfect person for me. It was hard to get a face to a name. Everywhere I looked, people were giving me little to no details, but I didn't give up. I kept going until I finally found someone that would point him out. I felt out Trey first by getting a few drugs for him. I needed to see how professional he was. When I saw how he handled the drug business, I knew I had the right man.

' Trey was right about how he killed people. He knew what he was doing when it came to murder. Now the police considered it a cold case. They had no leads. The only thing they had was that it was a robbery. No witnesses came forward saying they saw anything. The case was over. And I'm out for the better.

"Now we are going to lower Brother Darius' body to ground. May he be one with the angels and in a place where he is alright and feels no pain. May he walk side by side with Jesus and into the light," the pastor said and it took everything in me to not laugh. Darius was nowhere up there with no damn angels. He was way downstairs with the demons in his rightful place. I wanted to scream that out loud but I bit my tongue. I was supposed to be the grieving widow.

I stood up and walked over to the casket as it was lowered. I grabbed one of the many white roses and I threw it over the casket. This ungrateful son of a bitch got what he deserved. After all I did for him, after all the years I put in, after everything, he still treated me less than shit. He cheated on me, took advantage of me, and lied to me. Never mind the fact that he wouldn't even have the business if it wasn't for me. He never cared about that; he just took whatever he could. Well who got the last laugh? He might have taken a lot of things from me, but I got to take his life. And that's something I don't really regret.

"No! No! No Daddy! Don't go." My daughter's voice screaming is the only thing that got me stressed. She was so devastated once I told her what happened to her father. She was asking where Darius was and I told her the truth. Usually when she asked that question, Darius was cheating, but this time he actually had an excuse; he was dead. I looked over at my mom trying to hold on to her, but my daughter was throwing a fit. She was crying and she was hysterical, and she was the only reason why I felt sad today.

I don't know how it's going to be to raise her without Darius. When I had her, that thought never crossed my mind. I just thought that he and I would raise her together, but that dream was as dead as Darius. Luckily for me I got all of his money, his properties, and half of his business, so I could at least take care of her financially, but what about emotionally? What about that?

Behind me sat Jamar. He actually looked a little sad and I suppose he was. Even with all the tension between him and Darius, they were really good friends at one point. He just sat there stone-faced the whole time. He didn't shed a tear, he didn't move a muscle, and it almost looked like he was barely breathing. When he saw me looking at him, he just gave me a small nod, then looked straight ahead. I suppose Jamar will help me raise my daughter. They are so close anyway, and he's always said he wanted to be a father. What better time than now?

Listening to my daughter wailing in the background made me misty eyed. The casket was almost completely down, and I shed a tear. Not because of Darius, no not at all, but for my daughter. This will surely change her life forever. She will never be the same, but with the support of Jamar and I, she will become strong. She will not let her father's death defeat her, but she will let it define her. She will somehow turn this grief into strength. I'll see to it.

The funeral ended and people started to leave. Everyone left me alone as I stared at the casket in the ground. My mom took my daughter and Jamar gave me space. It was just me and the casket. Pretty soon, they started to throw dirt on him. I put the black veil over my face and watched them. They too must have thought I was grieving, but I was actually hiding the smile that was on my face.

Jayla

I finally unpacked the last box. After a month of living in Houston, it was official, I am really a Houston resident. I thought it would be a drag to be in Houston, starting all over, but as soon as I got here, I felt an instant relief. There was no more drama and it felt so nice. Even Keon was different. After a week of being here, he enrolled himself in some classes at the local community college. Everything was changing, but it was all changing for the better.

Now that all the drama was back in Atlanta, it was like I was finally living. Everything that held me down was now gone. There was no Shenice. There was no Jamar. There was no hit man. Things would only get better.

My phone vibrated and I smiled when I saw Charmaine's number.

"Yes...." I was already giggling.

"Girl, we missed our flight," she said sadly.

"What?" I instantly got pissed. "See, this is why I wanted to call you and make sure you got up for the flight. But what did you tell me, you told me that you could make it. I'm so fucking mad at you."

"Damn girl are we friends or lesbians lovers?" she started laughing. Once she was laughing like that, I knew she was joking. "You know damn well I'm not missing no flight. You know they don't do no damn refunds and with my ass being hella cheap, I'm going to make sure my ass is in my seat on time."

"Oh gosh." I knew her rant was only getting started.

"And did you know that the flight attendant had the nerve to not give me a full can of soda. Now I get why they don't hand it to you, but why not pour me out my two cups? Doesn't my ticket pay for a full can?"

"Hey girl," Kim must have snatched the phone from Charmaine. "We are on an Uber, we'll be there in twenty minutes."

When I saw my two friends lugging their suitcases up to my place, I immediately ran out to hug them.

"Damn girl, it's only been a month," Charmaine laughed. They both wrapped their arms around me and I helped them into my house.

"So what do you guys think?" I asked them after I gave the small tour of my two-story four-bedroom, two-bath house.

"It's gorgeous," Kim complimented. "It's really coming together nicely."

"Thank you. I finally start work in a week, so I just took all that free time to concentrate on the house. I'm glad you like it."

"Where's the alcohol?" Charmaine whined. "I need to feel a buzz, I've had a long day."

After they settled in, they caught me up on all that was happening back in Atlanta. Nikki was hiring someone new to replace me. They weren't so happy about that, but seeing me here in Houston, they were soon getting over it.

"I do miss you," Kim brought up.

"Yeah me too," Charmaine added. "But damn, I can't lie, you look really happy." She had a sly smirk on her face.

"What is it now Char?" I rolled my eyes.

"Who is it?"

"Who is what?"

"The man that you obviously are seeing."

That's when I laughed like she was Kevin Hart, Eddie Murphy, or Chris Rock.

"Damn, it's not that funny," she pouted.

"Oh yes it is," I laughed. "It's funny because I'm seeing no one. I've really been here just fixing up the house. You guys know that a break is coming up soon so I will finally see my little sister. I don't have time for no dates." She gave me a look like she didn't believe me. "I'm being honest. I'm not dating anyone."

"Have you even thought about it?" Kim asked.

I got quiet. Ever since Darius died, I really didn't think about dating. In a lot of ways, I was still getting over him. We didn't break up, he died, and that was a lot to get over.

"No," I told them truthfully. "I'm really going to concentrate on me and my family right now. My sister will be here for the break and my brother is finally doing right. All me and my brother do is spend the day laughing and hanging out. I'm really grateful for him because I don't know how I would have made it without him. He's like my rock out here."

"That's good to hear," Charmaine smiled. "I'm happy for you."

"Me too," Kim grinned right along with her. "And don't be alone forever. If you want, you can go back out there and date."

"I'm not in any rush. I'm just looking forward to my new life," I informed them, but then I took a deep breath. "But if I do date, I have one rule."

"What is it?" they both asked at the same time.

"No more married men," I smirked. "Too much drama."

We all chuckled. I got out a bottle of wine and started pouring into their glasses.

Chapter 8

Jamar

I packed up the last things in my old office. I was moving into a bigger one. In fact, they knocked down the walls in Darius' old office to build mine. It was wider and will help me better handle the real estate and marketing. I made room for my assistant, because I wanted him near me. He told me he wanted to learn the business and it's time that he did. He was with the other sales agent taking notes, while I finished up things in here.

These past few months have been a whirlwind to say the least. First off, I never expected to fall in love with Shenice. Honestly, I thought that I would get a version of her if I was lucky, but never actually her. I use to tell Darius that Shenice was a good woman. She had done so much for him, and he took her for granted. I mean, I wasn't no angel myself. I had plenty of women, everyone here in Atlanta knows that, but I never had a woman like Shenice. She is the type to see your potential and make sure you make something of it. Maybe that's what Darius' problem was. Maybe he didn't like the fact that he owed Shenice a lot, so he cheated.

When Shenice and I first started out, I knew it wasn't going to be some fling. I've had flings before and usually right after sex, you just want to go home. But after I had sex with Shenice for the first time, I couldn't get enough of her. I thought she wouldn't feel the same, but luckily she did. So we went from screwing to falling in love in a matter of seconds. Maybe we were always in love. We did always have this playful flirtatious relationship. Who knew after all these years, there was a real love underneath it all?

Us finally being together wasn't the neatest or the easiest of situations, but we were making it work. After the funeral, Shenice and I promised to put it all behind us. The whole thing with Darius was now our past. There was no point in talking about it anymore; there was no point arguing about it anymore either. What's done is done and that was it.

"Okay sir," my assistant came up to me with a legal pad, "I just spoke to the movers, and they will have the rest of your things in by the end of the day. Would you like to stay here and watch them?"

"No, you can oversee that," I told him taking a few things from my office and tossing them in a bag.

"I'm going to be heading home." I held the small black plastic bag in my hand. "Tomorrow morning at 9 a.m. sharp we start. We're going to go over some marketing strategies and then we're going to go look over some listings."

"Okay sir."

"Are you sure that you're up for this work?"

"Yes sir."

"Good, because once I get started there is no slowing down, at all," I warned him. "You said you wanted to be in this business, tomorrow you're going to prove if you are a man of your word."

"Thank you sir. I won't disappoint you."

I nodded my head and left the office. All the workers smiled and said hi to me. The transition from me being a fellow worker to their boss went very smoothly. I guess it was because I was always handing out the rules and regulations when Darius wasn't around. People didn't seem to resent me or give a hard time. I was always looking forward to coming to work, and my staff was the main reason why.

At first taking on the sales part of the business was a challenge. I was used to being behind the scenes. I never talked or dealt with the clients. That was what Darius did. He handled the headaches and I handled how to get people in. But when I started doing both, it wasn't easy at all. The parts that I thought would be simple were not. I could see what Shenice warned me about. She trained me for the real estate part of the business. She made sure to hammer into my head the meaning of good customer service. She told me that I had to give them my all. I had a cell phone just for them. The second it rang I picked it up. I didn't matter what time of day it was, if I was awake, I was answering. Some of the clients took to me instantly. They liked me a lot and recommended other friends and family to me. The other clients, however, made me work hard. They called whenever, dropped houses because they didn't like the smallest detail, and they had some of the most ridiculous standards. I didn't give up though, with Shenice's help, I managed to take care of it all.

Driving my car down the highway, I couldn't wait to get home. My office wasn't the only new space. Today I was also moving into a new home. I saw the moving truck outside a gorgeous home. It was practically a mansion and I couldn't believe I got to call that place home now. The big trees, the huge yard, and the swimming pool, looked so dreamy. Shenice was outside being the boss that she was, telling the movers where to move my things. As I watched her move gracefully, I shook my head thinking how Darius could fuck this up. How could he not see the treasure that he had? I'm not going to make the same mistakes that he did. I'll forever cherish her, like he always should have.

Shenice

"What is that?" I walked over to Jamar and pointed at the small black plastic bag in his hand.

"Just some stuff," he said casually, but he was playing around. I knew it was something that I was going to hate. All day I had to put up with his too masculine stuff. He had a deer head, football helmets, and even a keg stand. What is it with men and those horrible things? Why can't some men be straight and have great taste in furniture?

"Uh uh. Open that up," I reached for it before he could open it to show me. It was some tacky football coasters of a team that I didn't know or care about. "Again with all these macho things. Why would you bring this here?"

"Because this is my home." When he said the word 'home' my heart just melted. He was right, this was his home.

I purchased this huge house with a chunk out of Darius' money. I figured I deserved it. It's a gated community right by Lake Lanier, so the scenery was gorgeous. The private school in the area is one of the best in the nation, so my daughter was learning from the best. On top of all that, it was tucked away. After Darius died, people felt like they could come over and pay their respects. Just because they saw the story on the news, they just wanted to see how I was doing. At first, I was cordial, but I grew sick of it. So the second the money cleared in my account, I was looking for a new home.

Another reason I left was I didn't want to be in that old home anymore. Not that I was haunted by Darius but I was haunted by the pain that was there. I was haunted by the fights I had with him The halls in my old house would have just reminded me of all the times I paced back and forth waiting for him to come home. The laundry room is where I would become a damn bloodhound because I smelled the perfume on his shirt, trying to see if it was mine or someone else's. The front window by the front door is where I was posted when I heard his car pulling up. The house was haunted with bad memories and bad vibes, and I wanted no part of it.

"So, how's the move coming along?' Jamar asked reaching out to hold my hand. It felt nice that he could do it all out in public and we didn't have to feel paranoid.

"Pretty great. Even though your things still look like they are for some bachelor, it goes well in our house."

"Say that again," he licked his lips looking seductively in my eyes.

"What? Our house?"

He grabbed me for a kiss and I felt myself fall in love with him all over again. He never hesitated to show in some way that he cared for me. This is how life should always be.

"I love you Shenice," he kissed my lips briefly.

"I love you, too."

We walked holding each other's hand, walking into our new house.

Epilogue

Trey

Now that all the drama was over, I was back in my business full time. My driver held me down so well, that I made him my partner. As his first test, he went to New York City to handle my disrespectful client. He sent me a picture of him bloodied up, and I knew I made the right decision. With the two of us working together side by side, nothing and nobody would stop us.

"Trey!" my boss called out to me. I walked into his office where he threw a duffle bag in front of me. "Do you know what this is?" he asked. I went to the bag and opened it up. It was filled with money. If I had to guess, I would say close to $100,000 in cash.

"Money."

"Yes, but this is your money."

I was confused. Of course I wanted to take it, but a good worker always ask why he's being paid for something that he didn't do.

"What's it for?"

"There are three snakes in my crew." My eyes opened wide. "That's right," he continued. "I have three snakes amongst me."

"Who is crazy enough to go against you?" I shook my head.

"I know but you know that I have a source in the DA's office and he told me their names. How would he know their names?"

"They'd have to be snitches." I took out my gun. "How do you want them ended?"

"You choose. I don't care if you shoot them in the head. I don't care if you stab them to death. Shit, I don't care if you kick them in front of a train, just get rid of them."

"Okay."

He smiled and then he handed me an envelope. I didn't have to open it to know what was inside. He probably put a picture, their known addresses and hangouts, and even their relatives.

"Here, use this burner phone so I can get in contact with you. When you are done text me the letter x. I'll know what it means."

"No problem. I got it."

This was a big difference from taking a job from a stranger. You had to do everything yourself and even then, you could make mistakes. Well I'm not doing that again. The next time a complete stranger comes up to me asking about my services, I'm going to deny them flat out. Shenice may have paid me well, but I could have gotten caught because of her. She was such a control freak, kinda like me, but she was sloppy.

"So you have your driver getting in on the action, huh?" My boss sat down behind his desk. I didn't ever tell him, but he had eyes and ears everywhere.

"Yeah, I got into a dumb situation and had to lay low for a while."

"How's he doing?"

"He's really good. He don't play when it comes to disrespect. Anytime he has to check someone, he'll call or text and ask how I want to handle it. He's really good."

"For you to say that, means you like him and like working with him."

"Nah, it's bigger than that, I respect him," I told him honestly. "Get gets the work done. He's reliable."

My boss nodded his head.

"One of these days I'm going to turn the business to you, that's no secret. You are one of my best workers. The money is always in on time and you get everything done. When I step down, I know that you are going to do a good job as my replacement. I don't have to be psychic to know that you won't disappoint."

"I won't," I replied confidently. He smiled and then sent me on my way.

I texted my new driver to meet me downstairs and he was on time. He would usually run two minutes or three minutes late, but now he knew to come early. He knew it was better to be early than late.

"Where too?" he asked. I pulled out one of the photos and saw that he was in Maryland.

"Take me to the airport."

He drove and I leaned back in my seat. I was glad to be working for my boss. If the assassination didn't come from him, I'm not doing it. I was done with all that extra drama.

My phone began to vibrate. I looked down and saw my old driver's phone number.

"What's up?" I asked him. "Are you there?"

"I just bought our plane tickets, both coach, and I'm waiting on you." I smiled when I heard this. He was so reliable. I was glad that I gave him more things to do because he was doing it well. My boss was right. One of these days, I'm going to run the business and he was going to be my right hand man.

"Good to hear." I ended the call and waited to be dropped off at the airport. Time to get back to work.

Shenice

Jamar was swinging my daughter on the swing set that was just installed yesterday. She was laughing and giggling without a care in the world.

"Higher!" she screamed.

"What's the magic word?" he laughed back.

"Please! Please Jammy!" She giggled some more.

The sound of her laughter and him going along with her put a smile on my face. It took a long time to get here, but I'm finally happy. My daughter is happy and every day she tells us that she loves us. She wasn't so weirded out with the change. It might have been because of how happy I am. Every time Jamar and I held hands, she ran up to us and held our hands too. We are a family now.

"Do you want to go down the slide?" he asked her.

"Yes!" she screamed. She got down off the swing and went towards the slide.

"I'm going to get you," he began chasing her and she ran with her pigtails bouncing on every step that she took.

"No Jammy," she laughed and they both fell to the ground. He tickled her and she screamed happily. She saw me and we locked eyes. She got up and hid behind me. "Mommy, stop Jammy."

Jamar came over pretending to be a monster. She was giggling and holding onto my thighs for dear life. They were so cute together.

"Mommy help me," she was still playing and hopping around.

"Mommy can't help you," he teased.

"Oh I can't?" I shot my eyebrows up. "I think I can take you on."

"Nope," he shook his head. "The only person that can help you is maybe a little brother or sister."

My heart started beating fast. The smile on my face and his face grew wide. I leaned in and kissed him.

"I want a little baby brother," my daughter said. "He'll be a baby."

"You want a baby brother?" I asked her.

"Yes," she nodded.

"And are you going to help Mommy with the baby."

"No, that's what Jammy is for," she said simply and ran around the backyard.

I shook my head and turned back to Jamar.

"You heard her," he laughed. "We got to get started on that baby brother."

"Are you sure that you want this?"

"I'm positive," he reassured me. "Let's have a baby."

"I suppose we have more than enough money to raise another child," I chuckled. "Okay."

Jamar laughed and then picked me up. He kissed me on the lips and then put me back down.

"Hey guess what?" he yelled out. "You're getting your little brother!"

"Yay!" my daughter screamed and ran up and hugged him.

"I love you," he kissed her forehead.

"I love you, too."

They walked in the house talking about baby boy stuff. I never thought I could be this happy.

Jayla

"Okay Keon, start from the top," I sighed rubbing my temples. "And try not to go too fast. Every time something gets you mad, you tend to speed up."

"I'm not mad. I'm just saying my professor is a bitch. He's not trying to work with me. You should hear him talk about his home, his car, and how one time he met Jennifer Lopez. The way he went on and on about it, you'd think they were fucking or something. And now he's trying to fail me."

"Wait, how did we get to you failing?"

Keon was two months into school and he already hated one of his professors. He was studying to be a pharmacy technician. He joked with all of his old friends pushing drugs; it would be nice for him to do it legally. I thought at first that it would be too much for him, but he took it seriously. Every time I came home from work, he was studying. He was either reading his textbook, going over his notes, or online looking up information. I was so proud of him. If only he could get along with that one professor.

"You don't have to love your professor Keon, just bite your tongue, and wait," I advised him.

"Wait for what? For him to get out of line? He's already done that."

"What did he do?"

"Just the way he looks at me."

I broke out in chuckles.

"You know what I think it is, you're not used to being in school so it's weird for you to take orders from someone else." He opened his mouth to argue but I started again. "What good will happen if you argue with him? What good will happen if you drop out? You're doing so well Keon, you really are. I mean look at where you were two months ago and look at where you are now. You're a better person and I'm proud of you."

He smiled when he heard me say that. I guess I don't say it out loud enough, but now I was. Keon wasn't running the streets and he was doing things to improve himself. I don't think of what might have happened if he didn't change. He might be dead like Darius, but he isn't. Keon is proof that people can change if they work hard enough.

"Okay, I won't let him get to me," he gave in. "Even if he deserves it, I won't knock him the fuck out."

"That's the spirit," I gave him an uneasy smile. "At least you're trying."

"Yeah I got it."

"Guess who is coming down to stay with us for a while?"

Keon smiled widely when he heard that. Like me, he loved and missed his sister. They were inseparable when we were growing up. It was going to be weird to see her after all these years. She wasn't going to be that young girl that went to boarding school; she was coming back a woman.

"I can't believe it. I can't wait for her to actually be here," he scoffed.

"Well you know you're going to have to look out for her. For all we know she might be boy crazy."

"Get the fuck outta here. Miss me with that bullshit please," he laughed. "If a nigga even looks at her, it's going to be a problem," he chuckled.

"So she can't even date?"

"Nope," he shook his head. "Not unless he graduated from Harvard or Yale or some other fancy college. Matter of fact..."

I listened to Keon go on and on about the rules and regulations that he was going to put down. He was so passionate about his little sister and it was nice to see that. Everything was falling into place. It's too bad Darius didn't live to see it, but Shenice wasn't going to let him slide. I guess in her eyes, his life was the ultimate price to pay for his sins.

~~~

Loved this series? Make sure you check out more of Mia Black's series listed below!

Taking What's Hers
His Dirty Secret: Charmaine's Story
His Dirty Secret: Kim's Story
Loving The Wrong Man
Love On The Low
Falling For The Wrong One
Her Addiction
Messin' With The Wrong One
His Obsession
Caught Up In Love

Follow Mia Black on Instagram for more updates: @authormiablack